This book belongs to

....

© 2008 by Parragon Books Ltd
This 2009 edition published by Sandy Creek,
by arrangement with Parragon.

Sandy Creek
122 Fifth Avenue
New York, NY 10011

ISBN 978-1-4351-1923-9

10 9 8 7 6 5 4 3 2 Lot
Manufactured 8/18/2010
Manufactured in China

The Velveteen Rabbit

Written by Margery Williams
Retold by Gaby Goldsack
Illustrated by Jacqueline East

Sandy Creek

Once upon a time, there was a Velveteen Rabbit. He was made from soft fur and he was stuffed with sawdust. He had thread for whiskers and his ears were lined with pink satin. When he was given to the Boy on Christmas morning, he was smart, chubby, and very, very cute. He was the best Christmas present.

At first, the Boy thought the Velveteen Rabbit was wonderful but then he put him away in the toy cupboard and forgot all about him.

The other toys looked down on the Velveteen Rabbit. They thought he was old-fashioned looking. Some of the more expensive toys ignored him. The only toy that was nice to him was the Horse. The Horse was the oldest toy of all and was very scruffy and worn. Unlike the other toys, he was REAL.

"What is real?" asked the Velveteen Rabbit one day.

"It's what you become when a child really loves you," explained the horse. "I was made real a long time ago by the Boy's uncle. It can take a very long time. By the time you are real some of your fur has dropped out. But it doesn't matter because once you are real you can't be ugly."

One night, when Nanny was putting the Boy to bed she couldn't find his favorite toy. She looked around and grabbed the Velveteen Rabbit by his ear.

"Here take your old bunny! He'll do to sleep with you," she said, putting him in the Boy's arms.

And from that night on, the Velveteen Rabbit slept with the Boy.

At first it was a bit uncomfortable. The Boy would hug him so tightly he could hardly breathe, and sometimes he'd roll over onto him. But soon the Velveteen Rabbit grew to love sleeping with the Boy.

The Boy and the Rabbit had great fun together. The Boy would talk to him in whispers and make tunnels for him under the bedclothes. And when the Boy went to sleep, the Rabbit would snuggle down beneath his chin and dream about becoming real.

The Velveteen Rabbit went wherever the boy went.

He had rides in the wheelbarrow,

and picnics on the grass.

He was so happy that he didn't notice that his beautiful fur was getting shabbier and shabbier, and his pink nose was getting fainter and fainter where the Boy kept kissing him.

One day, the Boy left the Rabbit on the lawn when he was called in for dinner. Much later, Nanny came to fetch the Rabbit because the Boy couldn't go to sleep without him.

"Imagine all that fuss about a toy," said Nanny, pushing the stuffed Rabbit into his arms.

"He isn't a toy. He's real!" cried the Boy. When the Rabbit heard these words he was filled with happiness. He was REAL! The Boy himself had said so.

Late one afternoon, the Boy left the Rabbit in the woods while he went to pick some flowers. Suddenly, two strange creatures appeared. They looked like the Velveteen Rabbit, but they were very fluffy and brand new looking. They were wild rabbits.

"Why don't you come and play with us?" one of them asked.

"I don't want to," said the Velveteen Rabbit. He didn't want to tell them that he couldn't move. But all the time he was longing to dance like them. He felt that he would do anything in the world to be able to jump around like they did.

One of the wild rabbits danced so close to the Velveteen Rabbit that it brushed against his ear. Then, he wrinkled up his nose and jumped backward.

"He doesn't smell right," the wild rabbit cried. "He isn't a rabbit at all! He isn't real!"

"I am real," said the Velveteen Rabbit. "The Boy said so." And he nearly burst into tears.

Just then, the Boy ran past and the wild rabbits disappeared.

"Come back and play with me!" called the little Rabbit. "Oh, do come back! I know I am real."

But there was no answer. The Velveteen Rabbit was all alone.

For a long time, the Velveteen Rabbit lay very still, hoping the rabbits would come back. But they never returned, and the Boy came and carried him home.

A few days later, the Boy fell ill.
His face grew flushed and he talked in his
sleep. Nanny and a doctor fussed around
his bed. No one took any notice of the
Velveteen Rabbit snuggled beneath
the blankets.

Then, little by little, the Boy got better.
One day, they let him get out of bed.

The Rabbit lay on the bed, as Nanny
and the doctor talked. They were going
to take the Boy to the seashore.

"Hurrah!" thought the Rabbit, who
couldn't wait to see the ocean.

Just then, Nanny caught sight of him.

"What shall we do with this old
Bunny?" she asked.

"Burn it," said the doctor. "It's full of
germs. Get him a new one."

The Velveteen Rabbit was put into a sack with a pile of garbage and carried to the bottom of the garden. The gardener was too busy to make a bonfire just then and said he would burn everything in the morning.

That night, the Boy slept in a different bedroom with a new bunny for company. It was a very fine bunny, with fluffy white fur and shiny glass eyes. But the Boy was too excited to think too much about it. All he could think about was the seashore.

Meanwhile, at the bottom of the garden, the Velveteen Rabbit was feeling very lonely. He wiggled around until his head poked out of the sack. He was very cold. His fur was so thin and threadbare that it no longer kept him warm. He looked around the moonlit garden and remembered all the fun times he had had with the Boy.

He thought about the wise and gentle Horse. He wondered what use it was being loved and becoming real if he ended up alone. A real tear trickled down his soft velvet cheek and fell to the ground.

Then, a strange thing happened. A tiny flower sprouted out of the ground. It was so beautiful that the Rabbit stopped crying. The petals opened and out flew a tiny fairy. She hugged the Rabbit and kissed his nose.

"Little Rabbit," she said, "I am the Nursery Fairy. When toys are old and worn and children don't need them any more, I take them away and make them real."

"Wasn't I real before?" asked the Rabbit.

"You were real to the Boy," the Fairy said, "because he loved you. But now you shall be real to everyone."

The Fairy caught hold of the Velveteen Rabbit and flew with him into the woods. There, wild rabbits danced beneath the silvery moon.

"I've brought you a new playmate," said the Fairy. "Be kind to him and teach him all you know." And she kissed the Velveteen Rabbit and put him down on the grass. "Run and play, little Rabbit," she cried.

The little Rabbit didn't know what to do. He had never moved before.
Then something tickled his nose and, before he knew what he was doing,
he lifted his hind leg to scratch his nose. He could move, and instead of
scruffy velveteen, he was covered in soft brown fur.

The little Rabbit jumped into the air and danced with joy. He really was a
REAL rabbit at last.